A NOTE TO PARENTS

One of the most important ways children learn to read—and learn to *like* reading—is by being with readers. Every time you read aloud, read along, or listen to your child read, you are providing the support that she or he needs as an emerging reader.

Disney's First Readers were created to make that reading time fun for you and your child. Each book in this series features characters that most children already recognize from popular Disney films. The familiarity and appeal of these high-interest characters will draw emerging readers easily into the story and at the same time support basic literacy skills, such as understanding that print has meaning, connecting oral language to written language, and developing cueing systems. And because Disney's First Readers are highly visual, children have another tool to help in understanding the text. This makes early reading a comfortable, confident experience—exactly what emerging readers need to become successful, fluent readers.

Read to Your Child

Here are a few hints to make early reading enjoyable and educational:

- ★ Talk with children before r⋯ ⋯ ⋯ ⋯ ⋯ ⋯ ⋯ ⋯ ⋯ ⋯ ich they already know about the Disn⋯ ⋯ ⋯ ⋯ ⋯ 'liar with the movie basis of a book, t⋯ ⋯ ⋯ ⋯ ⋯ e cover and some of the illustrations t⋯ ⋯ ⋯ ⋯ ⋯ is important, since oral language prec⋯ ⋯ ⋯ ⋯ reading.
- ★ Run your finger along the text t⋯ ⋯ ⋯ that the words carry the story. Let your child read along if she or he recognizes that there are repeated words or phrases.
- ★ Encourage questions. A child's questions are good clues to his or her comprehension or thinking strategies.
- ★ Be prepared to read the same book several times. Children will develop ease with the story and concepts, so that later they can concentrate on reading and language.

Let Your Child Read to You

You are your child's best audience, so encourage her or him to read aloud to you often. And:

- ★ If children ask about an unknown word, give it to them. Don't interrupt the flow of reading to have them sound it out. However, if children start to sound out a word, let them.
- ★ Praise all reading efforts warmly and often!

—Patricia Koppman
Past President
International Reading Association

For P. S.W. — M. H.

For Gaetan & Olivia — P. W. B.

*Special thanks to
Brent Ford and Adrienne Brown,
Disney storybook artists,
and Shi Chen*

102 Dalmatians is based on the book *The Hundred and One Dalmatians*
by Dodie Smith, published by The Viking Press.

Printed in the United States of America.
First Edition

1 3 5 7 9 10 8 6 4 2

The text for this book is set in 20-point New Century Schoolbook
Library of Congress Catalog Card Number: 00-105968
ISBN: 0-7868-1479-9
For more Disney Press fun, visit www.disneybooks.com

Disney's 102 DALMATIANS

Where's Oddball?

Written by
Mary Hogan

Designed by
Paul W. Banks

A Disney First Reader

Disney
PRESS

New York

**Little Dipper and Domino
are looking for Oddball.**

Where is that pup?

Oddball loves spots.

But her brothers can't spot her.

Domino meets Chomp.

"Where is Oddball?"
asks Domino.

Chomp saw Oddball
a moment ago.

But he does not see her now.

Little Dipper meets Drooler.

He asks, "Do you know where Oddball is?"

Drooler does not.

Domino meets Digger.

"Is Oddball here?"
asks Domino.

Digger shakes
his head.

Little Dipper and Domino meet Fluffy.

"Have you seen Oddball?"
ask Little Dipper and
Domino.

Fluffy has not.

How will Little Dipper
and Domino find Oddball?

Domino has a plan.

Little Dipper and Domino
lay out a trail of treats.

They wait for Oddball
to find them!

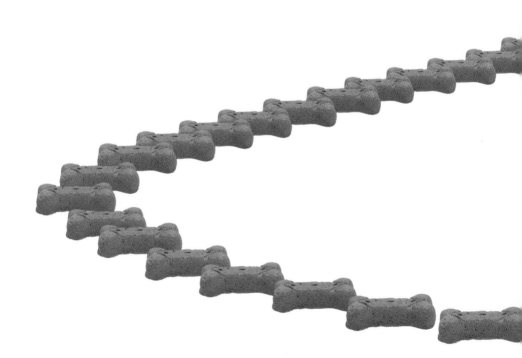

They wait for a long time,
then they hear...

CRUNCH-CRUNCH-CRUNCH.

Here comes Chomp.

Chomp and the pups wait
for Oddball. They hear...

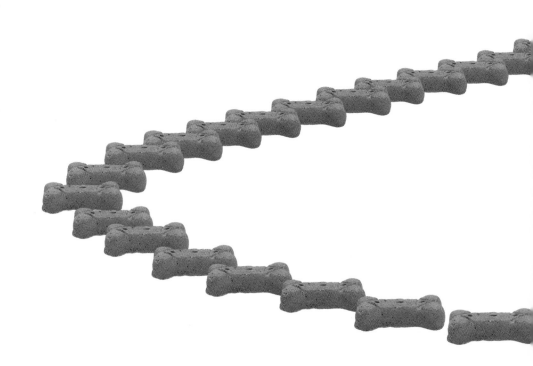

CRUNCH-*slurp~slurp.*

Here comes Drooler.

**Now four dogs wait for
Oddball. They hear. . .**

CRUNCH-**MUNCH-MUNCH.**

Here comes Digger.

Five dogs wait for Oddball.
They hear a small sound. . .

CRUNCH-CRUNCH-CRUNCH.

Here comes Fluffy.

**"Where can Oddball be?"
asks Digger.**

Fluffy looks at the treats.

"I've spotted the problem," he says.

The dogs lay out a new
trail of treats.

They wait for Oddball
to find them.

CRUNCH - CRUNCH - CRUNCH.

"SURPRISE!"

"I found you!" says Oddball.

   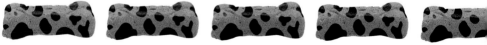

Woof!